A FEW THINGS YOU SHOULD KNOW ABOUT THE WEASEL

ALSO BY DAVID STARKEY

Starkey's Book of States (Boson Books, 2007)

Adventures of the Minor Poet (Artamo Press, 2007)

Ways of Being Dead: New and Selected Poems (Artamo Press, 2006)

David Starkey's Greatest Hits (Pudding House, 2002)

Fear of Everything (Palanquin Press, 2000)

Open Mike Night at the Cabaret Voltaire (Kings Estate Press, 1996)

A FEW THINGS YOU SHOULD
KNOW ABOUT THE WEASEL

A FEW THINGS YOU SHOULD KNOW ABOUT the weasel

POEMS

David Starkey

BIBLIOASIS

FIRST EDITION

Library and Archives Canada Cataloguing in Publication

Starkey, David, 1962-
    A few things you should know about the weasel / David Starkey.

Poems.
ISBN 978-1-897231-89-0

    I. Title.

PS3569.T335815F48 2010   811'.54   C2010-900985-1

Readied for the press by Eric Ormsby

PRINTED AND BOUND IN CANADA

For Sandy

Not a whisper, not a thought,
Not a kiss nor look be lost.

—Auden

Contents

I. Will

Q. Did Adam display free will when eating of the Tree of Knowledge?

A. That depends on whom you ask. Hegel was said to be famously bored by the question. Aquinas, in contrast, could hardly think of anything else. In all his voluminous writings, Aristotle, strangely, seems not to have mentioned the First Man at all.

Q. Does Aquinas attribute spontaneity or autonomy to the will?

A. Aquinas is rather too preoccupied by the Almighty to take that tack.

Q. Have you noticed how frequently Schopenhauer returns to the idea that our individual wills can lead us to the Kantian *Ding an Sich*?

A. Yes, he seems to be obsessed by the topic.

Q. Does Freud use the word "will" when analyzing voluntary movements in ideo-motor terms?

A. No, but William James does; he calls this mental picture a "kinaesthetic image."

Q. Do animals have free will?

A. No, they do not.

A Few Things You Should Know about the Weasel

It conceives at the mouth. The jack sticks
its long wet tongue down the doe's throat.
A few months later, she gives birth

through her ears. A kit whelped
from the right ear will be a buck;
the left's a bitch. A group of weasels

is called a gang. Skilled in medicine,
they revive their freshly killed young
with herbs. They carry the dead

they cannot save on their backs
and bury them in weasel cemeteries.
Above all, they stink. The once proud

basilisk, famed in myth and song,
became extinct after long exposure
to the feculence of weasels, a smell

so foul that Pliny the Elder and Isidore
of Seville vied with one another
to describe its stench in epic similes.

Jamestown

O America, let us celebrate
      your miserable beginnings: this feeble fort

           thrown up on the banks of a foul, salty
    river by adventurers hoping to cash in

on a New World they thought would forfeit
      its treasures as easily as the whores

         of Southwark's stews surrendered
   their sweet goods. It didn't work that way. Gold

was not forthcoming. Imported vines perished,
      silkworms shriveled. In their damp lean-tos

         the alien men and their few tattered
   women faced winter and typhoid fever,

dysentery and sloth. The natives were equally
      unimpressed by the thatch-roofed church

        and the invisible, nugatory god
   who ruled it. Yet it was here, brooding

by his fire, that John Smith intuited
      the meager necessities of empire.

        Taking stock of his assets—certain numbers
  of dice, colored beads, musket and cannon—

he realized that as long as a single
      Englishman remained alive

        to dream of pillage, no kingdom of mere
savages, whether noble or bloodthirsty,

could long endure. Tapping out the embers
        of his clay pipe, he strolled to the bulwarks.

           Somewhere beyond that forest of tupelo
    and tall marsh grass awaited a land so ripe

for the fucking that beneath his rusted armor
        the Captain, who had beheaded Turks

           and skewered pirates, who thought he'd never
    be o'erwrought again, was strangely stirred.

Waiting for a Train, 1929

The dance hall girls work the room for dimes
and drinks—and maybe something else.
A Real Gentleman from Back East proposed
marriage last month, so everyone's alive
with possibility: extra rouge and lipstick,
a new feather for the hat.
                                    But this bucko
from Cheyenne gets too drunk and gropes
his dame, then two jaspers from Medicine Bow
start a ruckus and the owner decides
to close the place down early that evening,
even though it's Saturday night.
                                    The girls
huddle around a table as the last joker's
chucked out in the snow. Irene
deals stud. Sheila brushes Ann Eva's hair.
On the phonograph, it's Jimmie Rodgers,
the Singing Brakeman, moaning
about not having a nickel, not a penny
he can show.
                        Ann Eva examines the coin
she's been rubbing between her thumb
and forefinger: Mercury's handsome puss
on one side, something like an ax
wrapped in olive branches on the back.
Heads, she's thinking, and she'll blow it
on a drink; tails she'll save it for her daughter
over in Scottsbluff.
                                    But she doesn't even flip.
It feels so nice what Sheila's doing that Ann Eva
waves to the bartender for a whiskey, Irene's voice
a glimmering aria to everything that's yet to go wrong.

Snapshot: Fort Worth, Texas

You'll wreck your womb,
you keep dancing like that,
the man with the stallion
tattooed to his bicep whispers
to her between songs
at the Borrowed Time Saloon.

But she plucks his hand
from her shoulder and digs
her boot into his shin,
sends him spinning to the floor.
Face bleach-white, forehead
slick with sweat, he stares

until her face, too,
becomes a mask. Her eyes
are the color of a whiskey
sour; his, obsidian.
For a moment, they're poised
on the pin-tip of violence . . . .

Then her friend, finished
heaving, make-up back
in place, breaks the spell.
She stumbles from the Ladies
Room, camera in the air,
hollering: *Everybody smile!*

My Parents' Bedroom

No TV on the dresser when I was growing up,
just a reading lamp on each side of the king-sized bed,
and stacks of shiny paperbacks: *North and South*,
Dune One through *Six*, *Everlasting Love*.

                                     Mom's polyester
pantsuits were color-coordinated in her closet,
while Dad's twenty pairs of ironed jeans hung
in one long row in his.
                    Everything
had its place, and I found no dark secrets rummaging
through their drawers when they weren't home—
no hidden *Playboy*s or strange sex toys, only his cloth bag
of poker money, mostly rolls of quarters, stashed
behind his socks.
                Their second-story window
looked out on our suburban street,
where one morning I parked my bike after finishing
my Sunday paper route. I'd locked myself out,
and when they didn't answer the door, I climbed the roof,
tapped the glass politely.
                  When they drew
the blinds, Dad stood there with a pistol,
ready, he later said, to fire.

Spring Flowers

I miss the comfort in being sad.
   —Kurt Cobain, "Frances Farmer Will Have Her Revenge on Seattle"

April 1994 and the children
of Seattle are bereaved.
The one man who seemed
really to understand them
has blown his brains out
with a shotgun. In flannel
shirts they gather to sing
his dirges, throw syringes
on makeshift altars of candles
and cards, Narcissus and daffodils.

Meanwhile, back in Rwanda,
where bullets are a luxury,
young men use clubs to cave in
skulls, machetes to hack off
arms and legs and heads. One
by one, those hiding in churches
are plucked from sanctuary,
marched to the cemeteries
and killed. Gladiolas flame
along the roadside in the rain.

In South Carolina, I brood
in my two-bedroom home
with my three children and my bi-
polar wife, mourning my own
miserable life through poetry.
Already it's ninety degrees
in the afternoon, dogwood
blooming, yellow jasmine
running up the phone poles,
tulips bursting as if from pain.

Yelling

Oh, when I think of all the places
my ex-wife yelled at me!
                    Throughout
the house: in the kitchen and
in the bathroom, in the living room
and on the stairs, in the basement
by the washing machine,
and standing by the bookcase, throwing
books and yelling.
                    She yelled
at the supermarket checkout counter
when I thumbed through a copy
of *Watch Your Weight*, and on the corner
of Randolph and Michigan
during the biggest blizzard
in fifteen years.
                    In the backyard,
her voice growing hoarse
and raw with the madness
her mother and grandmother
and great-great grandmother
bequeathed to her, she yelled
until the neighbors looked over
our rickety back fence
(then she yelled at them
for listening).
                    In the car,
especially in the comfort of the car:
on a five minute trip to Burger King
or a ten hour drive to another
state. She yelled about the traffic
and her grievances at work
and what I had or hadn't done
that day.

She bitched and belly-
ached, she fretted, carped and groaned.
She delivered tongue-lashings
and gave everyone every last
piece of her mind. She bewailed
and bemoaned her treatment
at the hands of strangers. She bellowed,
griped, groused and grumbled.
She even kvetched
occasionally, but primarily
she yelled.
        She yelled at midnight
and at midday and
in the twilight—nothing about her voice
the slightest bit crepuscular.
She yelled at noon and
in the afternoon and early
in the dawn, before the stars
had faded, before I'd fully
come awake.
        From what I hear,
she's doing fine without me
there to listen, alone in the house
I gladly signed away, alone
with the wide world that made her
so desperately unhappy,
alone, alone but yelling still . . . .

A Very Rich Old Woman

My sons and grandsons greeted my demise
with glee, though they were politic enough
to mute it at my memorial. Inside,
they bubbled with plans: new Jags,
the latest Rolexes. They daydreamed
of gorgeous, irresponsible women
impossibly contorted on heart-shaped beds.
Men's money cravings are different
than women's.
           I know.
              Secretary
to a great man, I married wealthy
in my twenties. It was security I wanted,
not show. Forty years my senior,
a grandfatherly old scamp,
he wasn't around for long. As decades
passed, I managed my interests well,
knew when to get in
and out of oil, had a knack
for high-tech stocks. I befriended
the right people. I listened
carefully. When it mattered, I held
my tongue.
           Hoi polloi
expect scandal from the great,
so I drank Screwdrivers for breakfast,
Bloody Marys were my lunch,
and by evening all I needed with my vodka
was a twist of lime. I bathed nude
on my private beach well into my seventies,
and seduced the local Monsignor,
giving him a new Mercedes every year.
None of it clouded my judgment,
and though they all said spiteful things

behind my back, no one ever returned
a penny of the money I spread around
like manure at planting time.
                              In accordance
with my wishes, they burned me,
scattering my ashes
from a plane over the ocean:
some of me sank straight to the bottom,
some of me was borne aloft on the breeze,
settling on the roof of the university library,
which bears my bountiful name.

Shelley in Santa Barbara

"Poets are the unacknowledged legislators
of the world," I tell my wife.
Eventide. We have been drinking
Chardonnay as the Santa Ynez mountains
fade to purple in the near distance.
Fog rolling in from the Pacific
obscures our Channel Islands view.

"What?" she says. I repeat the claim—
"Shelley's idea," I tell her, "not mine."
Two mourning doves slice
down the canyon, angle toward us,
barely clear the roof.
                        Next door,
the two normally sedate lawyers
are throwing a party. "Timber!"
someone yells, and something crashes,
though not a tree, I'm sure—
the Neighborhood Association
would not approve.
                        My stepdaughter
steps out back to borrow fifty dollars
for a movie, and my wife forks
it over.
            "My Bentley!" someone screams
at the party, and everyone howls.

The doves return, alight, take wing again.

"Poets are . . ." I begin once more, but my wife
holds up her hand: a warning.
"Not in *this* world," she states flatly,
refilling her crystal goblet almost to the rim.

Promises, Promises
   —For S.

The question, emailed from someone I don't know,
      nevertheless looms large: *Dream to be a hero
         in her bed?* Of course, I do—this is my wife
            we're talking about. How could I fail

to be interested in the elaborate
      and ungrammatical come-ons: *Enlarge
         you're banana length! Don't loose your passion
            to bad potence! Get ready to the wildest nights*

of your life with the original blue-pill!
      Yes, she tells me there's more to marriage
         than physical love—taking out the trash,
            for instance, vacuuming and laundry

and picking up after our St. Bernard—
      but surely my satisfactory discharge
         of those domestic duties must pale beside
            a gratifying boosted performance like Mr. Sex Machine!

What minor miscalculation wouldn't
      she forgive—the compliment paid too late,
         socks left in the living room, the cable bill
            overdue again—if only I could lead her

into *a world of boundless enjoyments,*
      where my *splinter will be bigger and more solid,*
         where *excellent hardness is easy* and I
            can *stay real man even being drunk.*

II. Form

Q & A: Form

Q. Did Kant believe that matter and form "lie at the foundation of all other reflection, so inseparably are they connected with every mode of exercising the understanding"?

A. Yes, he did.

Q. Was Locke skeptical of inquiries after "substantial forms"?

A. Yes. He regarded the entire subject as "wholly unintelligible."

Q. Are size, shape, color and weight generally considered "accidental forms"?

A. Actually, Bertrand Russell, who relished making pronouncements about physics and art, argued that form is simply a kind of "accidental style."

Q. Does Christian theology concur with the Platonic theory that Ideas are the eternal models or patterns for forms themselves?

A. It depends on whom you ask. The profound mystery of the creative act is either performed with God's blessing, or it is the cunning handiwork of Satan. Among the cognoscenti, there seems to be relatively little middle ground.

Q. Can controversies about form be distinguished from formal controversies?

A. Of course. Have you heard the one about the psychologist and the epistemologist who go into a bar? The psychologist orders a Lime Rickey, "with a twist of theology." The epistemologist orders a Fish House Punch, "hold the first principles." You can guess what happens next.

The Women of Lucas Cranach the Elder

They do odd things with their hands.

*

As though fingers were appendages for which our species had not quite learned the proper use.

*

Whether they are nude or clothed, their expressions often remain impassive: eyes narrowed, lips pressed shut.

*

When they do smile, they don't mean it.

*

Not really.

*

Judith with the bloody head of Holofernes looks pretty much like Eve, who is largely indistinguishable from Venus or Diana or the Princesses of Saxony.

*

Women, we are to understand, need do little more than focus hard on the what-comes-after.

*

Often they gaze down and away from the painter.

*

God knows what they see there.

*

Possibly an unsatisfactory glimpse of eternity.

*

Dirt, more likely.

*

Or a rat poking its snout from a hole.

*

This *is* Germany during the Reformation.

*

Ac sic magis per multas tribulationes intrare celum quam per securitatem pacis confidant.

Cuckoos

We Americans are all cuckoos. We make our homes in the nests of other birds.
—Oliver Wendell Holmes, 1872

summer is a-coming in
    the tune twittering
  from pan pipes carved out of someone's
    borrowed bones

  hammering and fishing
    fishing and hammering

        house-hunting

    roustabouting

old shoes with old holes in their soles

    a drunkard
  wallowing in muddy memories

demons sleeping in subway seats

  two girls comparing notes
    in the ladies room
      while their dates
    contemplate

  the old switcheroo
    the old bait and switch

a fiddler scraping
  "See That My Grave Is Kept Clean"
    in the rubble of the bombed-out building

ashes mixing with the rosin
    on his untuned strings

Hitler's Art

I hate to admit it, but he wasn't bad.
    No Feuerbach, sure, but you recognize
        the Karls Church in winter, St. Stephen's spire.
The mountain lakes, the castles ringed
    by quaint villages are places you might visit

on summer holiday. Landscapes
    were his specialty, watercolors
        his most effective medium. He learned
the knack of when to lift the brush and when
    to let the pigments blend. He couldn't, however,

draw a human face to save his life.
    The best student in any eighth-grade class
        has more command of nose and mouth, has more
insight. A realist and a classicist,
    he painted what his patrons craved and took

the best prices he could get. Sometimes,
    when I listen to Elgar's Cello Concerto
        in E Minor, written the year after
the first war, I imagine Hitler beginning
    to sketch swastikas in earnest. I think

of Elgar losing his wife, then fourteen
    barren years to death, while Hitler's craft
        increased. And I feel that I understand
the difference between architecture
    and art, between exactitude and—say it—*soul*.

A Brief History of Twentieth-Century Architecture

The world, at first, was proud of itself, vast
expositions and fairs, miracles
of Industry.
        Then the Soviets, their sly
flirtation with the avant-garde, and American
skyscrapers built on breadlines.
                      Not to mention
Albert Speer and his Nazi Vatican.

The *volta* came after the War,
                   prefab
Levittown, and all the concrete, steel and glass
it took to resurrect London, Leningrad,
Hiroshima.
        Postmodern
was merely a term coined to camouflage
the fear everyone felt—we have it still—
that every building standing was just a dry run
for something bigger, worse:
                    the opposite of *build*.

Notes for a Novel to Be Set in Myrtle Beach

A general aura of good times not had,
    fast-food joints and souvenir stands
      on bright, empty Sunday mornings.

End Time churches with their parking lots full.
    A plot against the liberal President
      by military men, retired insurance agents

from the even deeper South. Burned up with luxury,
    they meet on the golf courses of affluent
      housing tracts—Quail Creek Plantation,

Garden City Shores—plan assassinations, bitch
    about their income tax. And neon, of course.
      Saturday night teenagers swilling beer

in video arcades. Fight on the pier. Rape
    on the moonless beach. Unlikely heroes: a dentist
      (allusions to *McTeague*) and a black mechanic

(avoid the obvious clichés). They stumble
    through a maze of clues: politicians,
      lifeguards, KKK and Young Republicans.

Uncertain ending. Is it the Colonel or
    the one-eyed bookseller? No one
      goes to jail. Winter wind whips the sand.

The Detective Novelist

He dims the lights as he types, wears
a porkpie hat, smokes Kamel Reds,

but he's never fired a gun,
only knows about criminals

through arrest affidavits, morgue
reports and other writers' books.

Sometimes you'll find him knocking back
drinks at Chili's or at Bennigan's,

scribbling down snatches of banter,
TV reflected in his specs.

But he avoids the lowlife bars,
preferring not to have his hat

handed to him by thugs, the likes
of which his readers say he draws so well.

His first wife left, called him a fake.
However, the second gets it:

Art and Life keep poor company.
She loves sitting in the living room,

sipping on a glass of Chardonnay,
listening to his fingers clack

against the keyboard. Suburban
calm outside—doves cooing, sunset—

while down the hall the hero pistol-
whips a whore, whacks his nemesis

across the jaw with a two-by-four
and stumbles home to the woman

who waits for him, no matter what
he's done, or who he claims to be.

Do Svidaniya

Three Russian émigrés at an outdoor restaurant.
Pacific Ocean, Butterfly Beach. Surge
of surf, nearby conversation muted.
On their table, the remains of breakfast:
egg scraps on plates, empty bread baskets,
four bottles of champagne. They share
the same father, but little else, and silence
has settled on them like coastal fog.

One is a professor of linguistics
at the local junior college. Each day
he fails at teaching sun-drenched morons
the simplest aspects of morphology.
Even syntax, even *phonetics*, for the love
of all things sacred, they cannot grasp.
He fiddles with his napkin, eyes darting
periodically to the waiter, anxious for an end.

The second's racket is "Imports/Exports,"
although his brothers hear rumors
of broken kneecaps and much worse.
Growing up in Leningrad, he was the loser,
but he's lounging now in a Dolce & Gabbana
pin-stripped suit, a pair of A. Testoni loafers
on his size-14 feet. If this weren't California,
he'd be puffing on a hand-rolled Cuban cigar.

The third brother is a poet with no visible means
of support, although he seems the most content
to let this stillness take its course. Indeed,
he's almost smiling. Palm fronds shimmering

in salty breeze, screeching gulls, valets
parking Jags and Aston Martins, the awkward
family situation there's no escaping—
this is the stuff from which he crafts his verse.

They have not been together for a decade,
are unlikely to meet again for years,
but sooner rather than later one of them
will stand, and then the others. They will kiss
on the cheek, shake hands all around,
say goodbye in their native language.
Just now, though, the dead air continues,
as they wait to be presented with their bill.

The Venus of Willendorf: Ottumwa, Iowa

She stands in line at the Dairy Queen,
thick-thighed, knock-kneed,
wide and sagging buttocks,
enormous breasts hanging over
her bulging stomach like two
half-inflated basketballs
resting on a witch's cauldron.

Skin-tight polyester pants,
T-shirt emblazoned with
"Don't Hassel the Hoff":
she's a different kind of primitive,
though this is the body
her European ancestors carved
from limestone twenty-one
thousand years ago. They knew
then what her stout farmer
husband and their three
chubby kids know today:
excess of flesh is cause
for celebration in a world
where flesh decays while stone
survives.
      As the five of them
take their plastic trays
of shakes and onion rings
and triple-decker burgers
to a booth, I pay silent homage
to this goddess of Wapello County:
totem, charm, harbinger:
sacred mother of all things.

Higher Education

The glaziers at the Cobbledick-Kibbe
warehouse were pretty evenly divided
about whether it was worth pursuing
any schooling beyond those first twelve years.

Union men, they reaped the benefits
of Local 718. Butch said it was better
to go to work right away. *Before you know it,*
you'll be a Journeyman, then a Master.

Chuck voted for college, wished he'd gone
rather than starting a family so young.
Get out and see the world, he said. *Them*
chances you lose, they don't come back again.

Johnny, his silver hair slicked back
in a pompadour, pack of Winstons rolled up
in his T-shirt sleeve, muttered: *Go to college.*
Just don't let it interfere with your education.

I thought of them today, decades later,
when I paused at a worksite downtown
to watch a glazier roll a cutter's wheel
across a pane of smoky glass. Mostly,

I have forgotten their paternal counsel,
though occasionally some sliver
of memory—a ribald joke, my teenage
reflection in a broken mirror—slices

through the present long enough to matter.
I nodded at the worker, then walked on:
I had a meeting to attend. The scrap
fell to the ground, but didn't shatter.

III. War

Q. Is Juvenal's remark that "we suffer the ills of a long peace" and that "luxury is more pernicious than war" slightly disingenuous?

A. Yes. Slightly.

Q. Does Augustine, in *The City of God*, "lament the necessity of just wars"?

A. He does. In response, Aquinas contends that for peace in general to exist, men must find concord within themselves: "for a man's heart is not at peace, so long as he has not what he wants." Aquinas also believed in stigmata, the intercession of saints, and the restorative power of hot eel's blood.

Q. When Hobbes equated anarchy with "the condition of war," was he writing from personal experience?

A. And then some. He came wawling into the world prematurely, when his mother was informed of the Spanish Armada's approach. "My mother gave birth to twins," Hobbes famously said, "myself and fear."

Q. Does Rousseau attribute the origin of war to defective interpersonal relationships?

A. No. Rousseau believes that war "is a relation, not between man and man, but between State and State." That said, Rousseau was known to be something of a belligerent himself, as for instance the time he hurled a large volume of essays at Diderot during a heated dispute about the entry in the *Encyclopédie* for "*Paix.*"

Q. Does William James find the human race as bellicose as its individual members are instinctively pugnacious?

A. Indeed, he was known to say that he would "fight to the death" in defense of what he called the "cash value" of his words.

My Life as a Shang Shih
—Henan Kingdom, 1220 BCE

First, we killed the tortoises.
I didn't like that part, too easy
                        to grab them, tickle their feet until
their heads poked out, then *slice*, and all that
            dark blood gushing. We gutted them
and prepared the shells, etching twenty
                        characters—long life and sudden death,
        wealth and poverty, peace
                        and war, good luck and bad—
from top to ass. The better part of our lives
            were spent that way, butchering
and scribbling. Occasionally,
                        after much ceremony, someone
        led the grandest landlords in.
                        They bowed; we bowed lower.
Smoke and flash. Finally, a bronze pin
            was taken from the fire and pressed
against the shell till cracks appeared,
            connecting war with fame, or love
        with poverty. The poor bastards
                    really took it seriously,
scurrying back to their palaces
            to revise their dearest plans, while we
sat around drinking rice wine, waiting
            to get the inevitable call
        for a new reading of the oracle.
                        Was it so much pigshit? Yes
and no. What does a tortoise shell

have to do with gods? And yet
who can predict their wills? No one.
So why not us as well as any
other? At least we gave fate an image.
At least we were men enough
to concede that the accidental
interaction of heat and bone
might be as practical as prayer.

Nineveh

—Stone tablets from the palace of Sennacherib, 7th century BCE

War, war—history is always war:
towers toppling, armies hauling off
the enemy's cattle, sheep and slaves.

Warriors: identical in shields and helmets,
spears held at the ready, scimitars
raised and slashing, daggers drawn.

For sport, there's lion-killing, hunting
wild asses. For religion, worshipping
colossal bulls sculpted from stone.

Palm trees stretch to the horizon, vine-
swathed oases burble in desert air—
this might be paradise,

but war is all that matters: ships hurrying
to battle, archers kneeling with quivers
full of arrows, mastiffs straining

against their leashes, snarling at the knots
of trembling prisoners, while clerks tally up
the loot: gold, captured gods, silk-sheeted beds,

and piles, neatly stacked, of soldiers' heads.

The House of Fame
—*Metamorphoses*, Bk. 12

In my insufficient bones, the rustle
of ruin. Folly curses the dog bites
of Fate. A clattering of trifles (or
is that *rifles?*)—old and new
bores buckling their pants
after another rape. No pardoning,
no grace in this reverberating tower.
Fame, that whore, sits smiling down
on all of us, channel-surfing from war
to gossip to royal marriages.
The thundering voices sound
so important, but listen carefully:
they're only echoes of echoes.
There's no news at the core,
only silence unwilling to be itself.

David
—*after Donatello's bronze*

This is what's sweetest about victory,
to strip down to nothing but your leather
boots and suave wreathed hat and *pose*: one hand
(still clutching the fatal rock) on jutting hip,
the other grasping a sword almost
too heavy to lift. The wind whispering
across your genitals feels soft
as freedom. And what is there for the gathered
crowd to say? Yes, they'd love to ridicule,
to hoot at your wry grin and hard nipples,
your total *savoir faire*, but they dare not
when you stand like that, one foot on the ground
you've made your own, the other on that grander
trophy, the bearded giant's severed head.

Birds of Prey: 1944

Mississippi Senators
harping about state
sovereignty.

An insufficient army sent
to shelter refugees huddled
on the Black Sea's shores.

Spitfires plummeting,
flying bombs.

The Little Prince
floating like a harmless
harrier above the sea.

And in Germany, gold
teeth vanishing
and the Ode to Joy.

Constantina: 1968

Her hair loomed as large as the draft laws.
      I never loved her, though I adored her, a thorny sort
  of worshipping. We met, coincidentally,
             outside a Fort Dix guard box. She had chained
herself to the left leg of Private Anderson;
    I was chained to his right. "Sweetness," I said,

as the billy club blows began to rain, "these geese
         in your eyes will migrate come fall." Already
  that first night out of jail,
         I could hear the sound of her dumping me.
She laughed: "I am often bored, so you
  will need to suffer. Often." I nodded.

Though her skin smelled of wet ivy,
      she was fire in all other ways. Red hair,
  voice clanging like a red engine tearing
        down a suburban street. The sulfurous taste
of her tongue, like licking an open matchbook.
  The soles of her feet, rough as matchsticks.

I tried, repeatedly, to reinvest myself in The Cause.
    "*À propos de bottes,*" she'd say, changing
  the subject. And: "You'll remember me."
      The last time I heard her voice
was on a yellow telephone. On TV,
  white crosses covered Harvard yard.

Hanging Out With Bosnians
(Detroit, Winter 1996)

This happened with my cousin Eddie,
  who seeks out the gloomy and oppressed,
   and these guys—
    man.

So we're sitting around this dude Šušak's place,
  five of them speaking some language
   nobody can understand, loading
    the bong with chronic,

swilling Schlitz, and it's just deadly.
  Hip hop playing over the Lions game.
   Finally, Šušak says
    he's got a joke.

It's about this guy in Sarajevo. His mother
  gets shot, then his sister takes
   a piece of shrapnel in the chest.
    He starts eating bark

and grass and building fires with his grandfather's books.
  Eventually, he lies down in the street.
   His friend comes up:
    "Hey, are you alive?"

Long silence. Šušak starts laughing
  like a motherfucker. The guy
   opens his eyes, says to his friend:
    "Not so you could tell."

Ax

Give a man an ax and get out of his way. He'll hew the palm trees on the Promenade and chop down his own backyard fence. He'll smash his son-in-law's violin. He'll wreck the piano in the school cafeteria and the one huddled, harmless, in the church. Sweat drips down his forehead. The sharp blade biting into wood sounds like an undiscovered mark of punctuation, something more cogent than our current "exclamation point." In the right man's hands, the heft of an ax-handle feels as certain as a steering wheel.

The Murder Suspect, Moments Before
He Is Confronted by Police

He sits in the driver's seat of a borrowed
Corolla, Red Sox cap tilted low over
his anguished face. Across the street, two cops
huddle together, whispering, gesturing
once in his direction—yet he can't find
the will to turn the key and pull away.
In the passenger seat, a Styrofoam
container of half-eaten beef chow mein,
cold rice stuck to the tines of a plastic fork.
The backseat is piled high with clothes.
In the glovebox, a loaded .38
snubby and half a box of cartridges.
He cracks the window to better hear the swish
of willow branches in the November wind.
There's a gingery taste on his mustache,
and he wipes it with his sleeve as a blast
of heavy metal erupts from a pickup
rumbling down the street. His fingertips
tingle—probably with cold, possibly
from something else. There's a needling twinge
above his heart, a flash of memory:
purple blouse, a braid of golden hair, a splash
of crimson on gray tile. The cops begin
to saunter over. Then, as he reaches
down, fumbling for his pistol, they run
toward him, guns drawn, shouting out his name.

Scientists Report

In Ice Age Mesopotamia
water
dripped from crevices,

brilliant birds
of scarlet and sulfur
flitted from one broad-

leafed tree to the next.
Pears grew ripe,
fell, and rotted on the ground.

Where now the air's
as dry as hatred,
fierce rain fell.

Good news
at last
from the front.

Assignments

Write a poem about the war:
Become the girl he left behind.

Write a poem about the war:
Become the guy he left behind.

Write a poem about the war:
Become the hardened enemy.

Write a poem about the war:
Become the God no one can see.

Write a poem about the war:
Take flight from battlefields, ascend.

Write a poem about the war:
As though the war would never end.

A Poem about the War

I've tried to get inside their skins,
the young men on the ground,

to stand inside the cargo holds of planes
up to my neck in coffins draped with flags,

to hold a child with her chin blown off,
or taste the dust and heat while slogging past

a severed foot half-buried in the sand.
But the corpses remain newsprint photographs,

images on my computer screen. Conscience
aside, the war is chiefly inconvenience:

higher gas prices, vague worries
when I board a plane. Oh,

and the veterans in my writing class,
with palpitations, confusion, forgetfulness,

nightmares, chest pain, shortness of breath
and uncontrollable crying—a long list

of symptoms they claim keeps them
from handing in their work on time.

IV. Eternity

Q & A: Eternity

Q. When Plato called the eternal "the world of the immutable" and the temporal "the world of generation," what was he thinking?

A. Plato's thoughts are as inexplicable as rose bushes in the rain. No one knows what he was thinking.

Q. Was Hobbes right to criticize the Scholastics for calling eternity "the standing still of the present time"?

A. Yes, he was.

Q. Which description of eternity is closer to the truth: "the white radiance" or "a many colored glass"?

A. Neither. Black dots on a field of black is closer to the truth.

Q. Do those who, on philosophical grounds, deny creation *ex nihilo*, also deny the world's beginning?

A. If they must. Epictetus thought pain was a mask. "Turn it and be convinced," he said. By this we are to understand that eternity is pretense, masquerade: God's inside joke on the Realm of Ideas.

Q. Is there a difference between "eternity" and "infinity"?

A. Look at it this way: sometimes the angels are called "metaphysical aberrations" by radical theologians. Other times they are called "the heavenly host," "the choir invisible" and "messengers of light."

The Place of Angels

According to Aquinas, one angel: one place:
one time
> Others disagreed

Seraphim & corporeality

The issue required centuries of careful pondering

Meanwhile, laborers piled one stone atop the next

> chapel into church
> church into cathedral

> thumbscrew & iron maiden
> stocks & brand & wheel

Beggars split open one another's skulls
for scraps of boiled meat

Undisturbed by earthly matters
> inside those cloistered studies
the real work went on, torchlight flickering

> scratch of quill on parchment

crossings out & celestial calculations

Angels hovered overhead
> absorbed in the revisions

implicated in the outcome
> of every wondrous word

St. Francis Disrobes

Angels come to him at Mass,
whisper of a Kingdom where
everyone's been stripped
of everything unnecessary.

He gazes out the window.
Only a moment ago, every creature
contested with its fellow
for a share of spoils.

But now, he steps out
into Assisi's public square.
Off come his shoes, his cloak,
his tunic and his hose.
He tosses his staff
onto the paving stones.

Let them all think he's daft—
the sun and breeze feel wonderful
on his bare skin, and already the ravens
are flocking to his outstretched arms.

The More Angels Shall I Paint

The more materialistic science becomes, the more angels shall I paint.
   —Edward Burne-Jones

And now these eggheads can map the entire sequence
        of chemical pairs that form the DNA
     of a human being—that former miracle—
can locate the birthplace of stars and track
   the paths of atoms. They can explain
       the very rise of life itself—another
     former miracle—and calculate numbers
so large that you and I cannot begin
   to pretend we can imagine them.

So what's left for faith when it's been left
       so far behind? Why, to do what it does best,
     of course: invent and ornament. We must
take up our brushes and render every last
   seraphim and cherubim and archangel,
       every warbling member of the heavenly choir.
   We must stipple and scumble and daub
each feather of Uriel's broad wings,
     each bloody nick in Michael's broad sword.

Thus shall religion and art, that stumblebum
       pair, triumph over anything so mundane
   as systematic study and the precise application
of facts. No, the world will always belong
   to the believers—not the knowers—we who need
       so little to sustain us in our credulity: an image
     on a canvas of a man with the forelimbs of a bird,
his halo made of nothing more than a little
   egg yolk and water mixed with flecks of gold.

Annunciation

Lately, angels have been appearing
in her bedchamber with alarming
frequency. She'll be chilling, surfing
the Web—minding her own business,
basically—when, suddenly, a little trill
of harp music: a visitor from Outer Space.

Sometimes their bodies are nothing more
than shafts of pulsing light, other times
they arrive accompanied by puckish
cherubs, adorned in robes of elaborate
brocade, full-on halos, their wingspans
wider than any goose she's ever seen.

Problem is, they don't say anything.
She's like, *Okay?* but they only hover there
above her iPod dock, as if whatever message
they've brought she's supposed to understand
already. She doesn't. Try talking to them
and they just smile, get all beatific.

Most people don't believe her, so she keeps
a box of stuff they've left behind. Feathers,
of course, lots of them, but also lilies that stink
if she doesn't toss them out. And then
these notes written in some crazy language
on thick paper that smells vaguely of cows.

Last night, a new angel came—bigger,
brighter, fierce. He brooded over her
for half an hour. Once she even thought
he'd slap her with those delicate hands they have.
She has a feeling this one will be back, soon,
with a question. And she'd better answer *Yes.*

Triolet: The Zaca Fire

The world will end this way: covered in ash.
Blackened trees pointing fingers at the sky.
    If God could see, he'd look down on us abashed.
The world will end this way: covered in ash.
    Some giant with a giant brush blackwashed
    The mountains—scent of soot, sable and lye.
The world will end this way: covered in ash.
Blackened trees pointing fingers at the sky.

The Death of Glenn Miller

These days, who ever thinks of him,
    that bespectacled bandleader who jammed
with the Andrews Sisters and sold
    Chesterfield cigarettes over the radio,
then joined the Air Force to bring swing
    to our boys in uniform? Jazz critics

deride his overly polished playing
    and pat orchestration, but your parents
and your parents' parents were wild
    for "Indian Summer" and "Tuxedo
Junction" and, especially, "In the Mood,"
    the perfect excuse to jitterbug away

their worries that Hitler and Tojo
    were about to terminate the good
times forever and dye the blues
    a permanent shade of deep indigo.
So what happened to his single-
    engine plane, which vanished over

the English Channel? Some say he was shot
    down by a British gunner that mistook
him for a Nazi Messerschmitt. Others
    claim he was whisked off to talk
the Germans into early surrender
    but was kidnapped and murdered

by the SS in a Paris brothel.
    Most likely, though, it was one of the one
hundred thousand bombs dropped
    over the ocean by an RAF battalion
returning from an abortive raid.
    Wrong place, wrong time: that old saw.

The nation mourned, of course,
   then the nation did what it does best:
forget. Meanwhile, your grandpa
   or your dad came home, balled
your grandma or your mom, bought
   a split-level and a lawnmower, ·

and went to work for the military-
   industrial complex. The years
evaporated or just turned stagnant,
   like water in a wading pool left out
all summer. Music changed.
   You knew you were getting old

if you still tapped your fingers
   to "Little Brown Jug." Finally,
all those boys whose moth-
   ravaged uniforms had long since
been tossed in the dumpster, began
   following Major Miller on that long

slow spiral from the cold night sky
   to the colder, blacker world below:
old soldiers surrendering up their war-
   worn souls to the lush orchestration
of oblivion, to the sweet yet melancholy
   strains of "Moonlight Serenade."

Surf's Up

The day she walked into the ocean
at Summerland Beach, they found
two newspaper photos taped above
her desk. The first was a Muslim man
caught in a frenzy of rioting Hindus.
Palms pressed together, head slightly
bowed, terrified eyes staring at the pistol
pointed at his head. The caption read:
"Despite his pleas for mercy, the man
was shot moments later." The second
was the Cone Nebula, a cloud of gas,
shaped like a sea anemone, speckled
with stars, twenty-five hundred
light years away. Her husband told
police she'd promised him the images
were talismans *against* despair:
it can end any moment; how lucky
we are to be alive in all this space.
But he acknowledged, too, she'd
always been something of a bullshitter.
"Bullshitter"—that was his word.
They never found the body, though he
walked the beach every day for a month.
The light there in late April is dazzling—
the air so blue it makes one dizzy,
and he remembered more than he cared to:
her crying jags, the way she'd placed
a scarf over her head and called it a shroud.
Once he spotted a sea lion savaged
by shark attack. Another day
it was the head of a pelican, its bill
pouch as soft as an old lady's skin.

Another Word for Snow

Nothing now for me here. April blizzard.
Milwaukee blanketed in white. Twenty-

odd old people scattered through the church strain
to catch the eulogy my brother delivers, which lasts

forty minutes, though I don't hear a moment
of love in all that biography: birth

dates, death dates and all the hard facts sandwiched
in between. Still, I don't do much better.

When I'm finished, the brief planting. Over
the open earth, a black canopy snaps

in the wind. A few more words, then the ancient
ones hurry to cars, their chief emotion

evidently relief at getting out
of the cold. My brother and I share a cab

to the airport, shake hands at the ticket
counter, check in for our separate coasts.

I drink three Scotch and sodas—she would not
approve—as the squall ebbs, runways are cleared.

When my plane banks above Cudahy,
there's a moment I think I see her resting place,

but a gust rocks the wings, we're caught
in clouds, and then, honestly, I don't know.

Acknowledgments

Thanks to the editors of the following journals, where some of these poems previously appeared:

Antioch Review: "The Detective Novelist"

Askew: "Ax"

Big Muddy: "Hanging Out with Bosnians"

Cincinnati Review: "David"

Clackamas Literary Review: "Venus of Willendorf: Ottumwa, Iowa"

Dos Passos Review: "A Few Things You Should Know about the Weasel"

Folio: "Scientists Report"

The Hat: "Notes for a Novel to Be Set in Myrtle Beach"

Lake Effect: "My Life as a Shang Shih"

Licking River Review: "Hitler's Art"

New Delta Review: "The Murder Suspect, Moments Before He Is Confronted by Police"

Panic Attack: "Birds of Prey"

Permafrost: "St. Francis Disrobes"

The Pinch: "The More Angels Shall I Paint"

Quarter After Eight: "Q & A: Eternity"

RE:AL: "Constantina, 1968"

Roanoke Review: "Snapshot: Forth Worth Texas"

Scrivener's: "A Brief History of Twentieth-Century Architecture"

Solo Café: "Surf's Up" and " Yelling"

South Dakota Review: "Surf's Up" (as "After Suicide") and "Shelley in Santa Barbara"

Subtropics: "Annunciation"

Tar River Poetry: "Another Word for Snow"

Teaching English in the Two-Year College: "A Poem about the War" and "Spring Flowers"

DAVID STARKEY is the poet laureate of Santa Barbara, California, and director of the creative writing program at Santa Barbara City College. Among his poetry collections are *Starkey's Book of States* (Boson Books, 2007), *Adventures of the Minor Poet* (Artamo Press, 2007), *Ways of Being Dead: New and Selected Poems* (Artamo, 2006), *David Starkey's Greatest Hits* (Pudding House, 2002) and *Fear of Everything*, winner of Palanquin Press's Spring 2000 chapbook contest. In addition, over the past twenty years he has published more than 400 poems in literary journals such as *Alaska Quarterly Review, American Scholar, Antioch Review, Beloit Poetry Journal, Cincinnati Review, Greensboro Review, The Journal, Massachusetts Review, Mid-American Review, Notre Dame Review, Poetry East, Southern Review, Southern Humanities Review,* and *Southern Poetry Review*. He has also written two textbooks: *Creative Writing: Four Genres in Brief* (Bedford/St. Martin's, 2008) and *Poetry Writing: Theme and Variations* (McGraw-Hill, 1999). With Paul Willis, he co-edited *In a Fine Frenzy: Poets Respond to Shakespeare* (Iowa, 2005), and he is the editor of *Living Blue in the Red States* (Nebraska, 2007). *Keywords in Creative Writing*, which he co-authored with the late Wendy Bishop, was published in 2006 by Utah State University Press.